BOOKNOTES

THE BOOKLOVER'S ORGANIZER

A special note of thanks to my patient and loving sister, Cheryl McLean, for her expertise about the world of bookmaking and for sharing it with me.

I credit the "ladies of the club" with the inspiration to do this book. Without the frustration of trying to keep track of all of their reading recommendations, it would never have become even an idea. Kate, Susan, Patty, Stephanie, Lisa, Kate, Holly, Anne and Sherry—thanks for the many good books, good talks and great company.

Much gratitude to my husband and best friend, Bob Tidwell, for his constant support, and to my sons Judd and Travis for their patience with my hours at the computer.

Thanks to my 'soul sister,' Barbara Scot, who always took time from writing her real book to ask after my project.

And thanks to my mom, Pat McLean, and sisters Carol Sutter, Shelly Pederson and Lori Forestelle for their everday love and support. I am blessed.

Jackson Creek Press, 1994

ISBN 0-943097-02-9

BOOKNOTES
THE BOOKLOVER'S ORGANIZER

Created by
Marilyn McDonald

Jackson Creek Press
Corvallis • Oregon

A Book of Verses underneath the Bough,
A Jug of Wine, a Loaf of Bread—&Thou
Beside me singing in the Wilderness—
Oh, Wilderness were Paradise enow!
: Rubaiyat of Omar Khayyam :

"Here's my small book out, nice and new, Fresh-bound—whom shall I give it to?"

—Cattullus
87-54 B.C.

 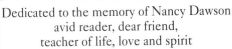Dedicated to the memory of Nancy Dawson
avid reader, dear friend,
teacher of life, love and spirit

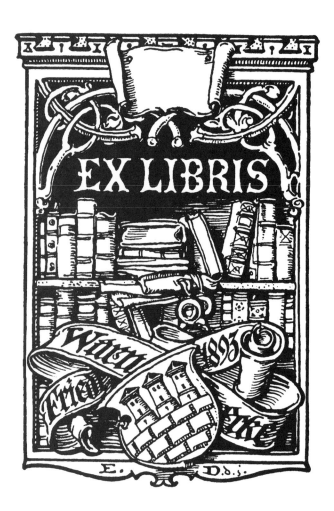

Contents

Loan Notes: *A tracking system for books loaned*

Book Notes: *Your personally annotated bibliography and book log, organized alphabetically*

Notes to Myself: *Blank pages for your own use—personal reflections, a chronicle of books read, booklists or reading goals*

Numbers of Note: *A phone list of your most-often-called book sources*

"Noted" quotes are sprinkled throughout for delight, enjoyment, and fellowship with readers past and present.

EX LIBRIS

ANTON PIECK

LOAN NOTES

Book Title	Borrower	Date Loaned	Ret'd

"Ever'thing comes t' him who waits but a loaned book."

—Frank (Kin) Hubbard

Book Title	Borrower	Date Loaned	Ret'd

Book Title	Borrower	Date Loaned	Ret'd

"When I get hold of a book I particularly admire,
I am so enthusiastic that I loan it to someone
who never brings it back."

 —Edgar Watson Howe

"Francie thought that all the books in the world were in that library and she had a plan about reading all the books in the world. She was reading a book a day in alphabetical order and not skipping the dry ones. She remembered that the first author had been Abbott. She had been reading a book a day for a long time now and she was still in the B's.... For all of her enthusiasm, she had to admit that some of the B's had been hard going. But Francie was a reader. She had read everything she could find: trash, classics, time tables and the grocer's list. Some of the reading had been wonderful; the Louisa Alcott books for example. She planned to read all the books over again when she had finished with the Z's."

—Betty Smith, *A Tree Grows in Brooklyn*

NOTES TO MYSELF

"*If you cannot read all your books...
fondle them—peer into them, let them fall
open where they will, read from the first
sentence that arrests the eye, set them back
on the shelves with your own hands,
arrange them on your own plan so that
you at least know where they are. Let them
be your friends; let them, at any rate, be
your acquaintances.*"

—Sir Winston Churchill

Date Read

Author _____ ☐ _____

Title _____

Referred by _____

Notes _____

_____

_____

_____

_____

Date Read

Author _____ ☐ _____

Title _____

Referred by _____

Notes _____

_____

_____

_____

_____

Date Read

Author _____ ☐ _____

Title _____

Referred by _____

Notes _____

_____

_____

_____

_____

Date Read

Author _____ ☐ _____

Title _____

Referred by _____

Notes _____

_____

_____

_____

_____

Author _____ □ Date Read ____

Title _____

Referred by _____

Notes _____

_____

_____

_____

_____

_____

Author _____ □ Date Read ____

Title _____

Referred by _____

Notes _____

_____

_____

_____

_____

_____

Author _____ □ Date Read ____

Title _____

Referred by _____

Notes _____

_____

_____

_____

_____

"*Wear the old coat and buy the new book.*"

—Austin Phelps

Author _____ ⬛ Date Read
_____

Title_____

Referred by_____

Notes_____

_____

_____

_____

_____

Author _____ ⬛ Date Read
_____

Title_____

Referred by_____

Notes_____

_____

_____

_____

_____

Author _____ ⬛ Date Read
_____

Title_____

Referred by_____

Notes_____

_____

_____

_____

_____

Author _____ ⬛ Date Read
_____

Title_____

Referred by_____

Notes_____

_____

_____

_____

_____

Date Read

Author _____ ☐ _____

Title _____

Referred by _____

Notes _____

_____

_____

_____

_____

_____

Date Read

Author _____ ☐ _____

Title _____

Referred by _____

Notes _____

_____

_____

_____

_____

Date Read

Author _____ ☐ _____

Title _____

Referred by _____

Notes _____

_____

_____

_____

_____

> "I *can't understand why a person will take*
> *a year to write a novel when he can easily*
> *buy one for a few dollars.*"
>
> —Fred Allen

NOTES TO MYSELF

"The peace of great books be for you,
Stains of pressed clover leaves on pages,
Bleach of the light of years held in leather..."
—Carl Sandburg

Author _____ ❏   Date Read
                                                              _____
Title _____
Referred by _____
Notes _____
_____
_____
_____
_____
_____

Author _____ ❏   Date Read
                                                              _____
Title _____
Referred by _____
Notes _____
_____
_____
_____
_____
_____

Author _____ ❏   Date Read
                                                              _____
Title _____
Referred by _____
Notes _____
_____
_____
_____
_____
_____

Author _____ ❏   Date Read
                                                              _____
Title _____
Referred by _____
Notes _____
_____
_____
_____
_____

Date Read

Author _____ ❏ _____

Title _____

Referred by _____

Notes _____

_____

_____

_____

_____

_____

Date Read

Author _____ ❏ _____

Title _____

Referred by _____

Notes _____

_____

_____

_____

_____

_____

Date Read

Author _____ ❏ _____

Title _____

Referred by _____

Notes _____

_____

_____

_____

_____

_____

"Always read stuff that will make you look
good if you die in the middle of it."

—P.J. O'Rourke

Author _____ Date Read

☐ _____

Title _____

Referred by _____

Notes _____

_____

_____

_____

_____

_____

Author _____ Date Read

☐ _____

Title _____

Referred by _____

Notes _____

_____

_____

_____

_____

_____

Author _____ Date Read

☐ _____

Title _____

Referred by _____

Notes _____

_____

_____

_____

_____

_____

Author _____ Date Read

☐ _____

Title _____

Referred by _____

Notes _____

_____

_____

_____

_____

Date Read

Author _____ ☐ _____

Title _____

Referred by _____

Notes _____

_____

_____

_____

_____

_____

Date Read

Author _____ ☐ _____

Title _____

Referred by _____

Notes _____

_____

_____

_____

_____

_____

Date Read

Author _____ ☐ _____

Title _____

Referred by _____

Notes _____

_____

_____

_____

_____

_____

> *"The walls of books around him, dense with the past, formed a kind of insulation against the present world and its disasters."*
>
> —Ross MacDonald

NOTES TO MYSELF

"Literature was not born the day when a boy crying 'wolf, wolf' came running out of the Neanderthal valley with a big gray wolf at his heels: literature was born on the day when a boy came crying 'wolf, wolf' and there was no wolf behind him."

—Vladimir Nabokov

Date Read

Author _____ ☐ _____

Title _____

Referred by _____

Notes _____

_____

_____

_____

_____

Date Read

Author _____ ☐ _____

Title _____

Referred by _____

Notes _____

_____

_____

_____

_____

Date Read

Author _____ ☐ _____

Title _____

Referred by _____

Notes _____

_____

_____

_____

_____

Date Read

Author _____ ☐ _____

Title _____

Referred by _____

Notes _____

_____

_____

_____

_____

Author _____ ☐ Date Read ___

Title _____

Referred by _____

Notes _____

_____

_____

_____

_____

Author _____ ☐ Date Read ___

Title _____

Referred by _____

Notes _____

_____

_____

_____

_____

Author _____ ☐ Date Read ___

Title _____

Referred by _____

Notes _____

_____

_____

_____

_____

"*It is a tie between men to have read the same book.*"

—Ralph Waldo Emerson

Date Read

Author _____ ☐ _____

Title_____

Referred by_____

Notes_____

_____

_____

_____

_____

Date Read

Author _____ ☐ _____

Title_____

Referred by_____

Notes_____

_____

_____

_____

_____

Date Read

Author _____ ☐ _____

Title_____

Referred by_____

Notes_____

_____

_____

_____

_____

Date Read

Author _____ ☐ _____

Title_____

Referred by_____

Notes_____

_____

_____

_____

_____

Date Read

Author _____ ☐ _____

Title _____

Referred by _____

Notes _____

_____

_____

_____

_____

Date Read

Author _____ ☐ _____

Title _____

Referred by _____

Notes _____

_____

_____

_____

_____

Date Read

Author _____ ☐ _____

Title _____

Referred by _____

Notes _____

_____

_____

_____

_____

*"In literature, as in love,
we are astonished at
what is chosen by others."*

—Andre Maurois

Notes to Myself

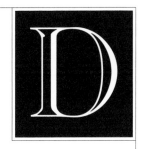

"*You think your pain and your heartbreak are unprecedented in the history of the world, but then you read. It was books that taught me that the things that tormented me most were the very things that connected me with all the people who were alive, or who had ever been alive.*"

—James Baldwin

Date Read

Author _____ ☐ _____

Title _____

Referred by _____

Notes _____

_____

_____

_____

_____

_____

Date Read

Author _____ ☐ _____

Title _____

Referred by _____

Notes _____

_____

_____

_____

_____

_____

Date Read

Author _____ ☐ _____

Title _____

Referred by _____

Notes _____

_____

_____

_____

_____

_____

Date Read

Author _____ ☐ _____

Title _____

Referred by _____

Notes _____

_____

_____

_____

_____

_____

Date Read

Author _____ ❑ _____

Title _____

Referred by _____

Notes _____

_____

_____

_____

_____

_____

Date Read

Author _____ ❑ _____

Title _____

Referred by _____

Notes _____

_____

_____

_____

_____

_____

Date Read

Author _____ ❑ _____

Title _____

Referred by _____

Notes _____

_____

_____

_____

_____

_____

"The man who does not read good books has no advantage over the man who can't read them."

—Mark Twain

Date Read

Author _____ ☐ _____

Title _____

Referred by _____

Notes _____

_____

_____

_____

_____

Date Read

Author _____ ☐ _____

Title _____

Referred by _____

Notes _____

_____

_____

_____

_____

Date Read

Author _____ ☐ _____

Title _____

Referred by _____

Notes _____

_____

_____

_____

_____

Date Read

Author _____ ☐ _____

Title _____

Referred by _____

Notes _____

_____

_____

_____

_____

Date Read
Author _____ ❏ _____
Title_____
Referred by_____
Notes_____
_____
_____
_____
_____

Date Read
Author _____ ❏ _____
Title_____
Referred by_____
Notes_____
_____
_____
_____
_____

Date Read
Author _____ ❏ _____
Title_____
Referred by_____
Notes_____
_____
_____
_____
_____

> "There are books by which the backs
> and covers are by far the best parts."
>
> —Charles Dickens

Notes to Myself

"Have you ever rightly considered what the mere ability to read means? That it is the key which admits us to the whole world of thought and fancy and imagination? To the company of saint and sage, of the wisest and the wittiest at their wisest and wittiest moment? That it enables us to see with the keenest eyes, hear with the finest ears, and listen to the sweetest voices of all time?"

—James Russell Lowell

Author _____ ❑ Date Read _____

Title _____

Referred by _____

Notes _____

_____

_____

_____

_____

Author _____ ❑ Date Read _____

Title _____

Referred by _____

Notes _____

_____

_____

_____

_____

Author _____ ❑ Date Read _____

Title _____

Referred by _____

Notes _____

_____

_____

_____

_____

Author _____ ❑ Date Read _____

Title _____

Referred by _____

Notes _____

_____

_____

_____

_____

Author _____ ☐ Date Read _____

Title _____

Referred by _____

Notes _____

_____

_____

_____

_____

_____

Author _____ ☐ Date Read _____

Title _____

Referred by _____

Notes _____

_____

_____

_____

_____

_____

Author _____ ☐ Date Read _____

Title _____

Referred by _____

Notes _____

_____

_____

_____

_____

_____

> "*Teaching has ruined more American novelists than drink.*"
>
> —Gore Vidal

Author _____ ❑   Date Read _____

Title _____

Referred by _____

Notes _____

_____

_____

_____

_____

Author _____ ❑   Date Read _____

Title _____

Referred by _____

Notes _____

_____

_____

_____

_____

Author _____ ❑   Date Read _____

Title _____

Referred by _____

Notes _____

_____

_____

_____

_____

Author _____ ❑   Date Read _____

Title _____

Referred by _____

Notes _____

_____

_____

_____

_____

Date Read

Author _____ ☐ _____

Title _____

Referred by _____

Notes _____

_____

_____

_____

_____

_____

Date Read

Author _____ ☐ _____

Title _____

Referred by _____

Notes _____

_____

_____

_____

_____

_____

Date Read

Author _____ ☐ _____

Title _____

Referred by _____

Notes _____

_____

_____

_____

_____

"People who like this sort
of thing will find this the sort
of thing they like."

—Book review by
Abraham Lincoln

NOTES TO MYSELF

"Books have always been living things to me. Some of my encounters with new authors have changed my life a little. When I have been perplexed, looking for something I could not define to myself, a certain book has turned up, approached me as a friend would. And between its covers carried the questions and the answers I was looking for."

—Liv Ullman

Date Read

Author _____ ⬛ _____

Title _____

Referred by _____

Notes _____

_____

_____

_____

_____

Date Read

Author _____ ⬛ _____

Title _____

Referred by _____

Notes _____

_____

_____

_____

_____

Date Read

Author _____ ⬛ _____

Title _____

Referred by _____

Notes _____

_____

_____

_____

_____

Date Read

Author _____ ⬛ _____

Title _____

Referred by _____

Notes _____

_____

_____

_____

_____

Date Read

Author _____ ☐ _____

Title_____

Referred by_____

Notes_____

_____

_____

_____

_____

_____

Date Read

Author _____ ☐ _____

Title_____

Referred by_____

Notes_____

_____

_____

_____

_____

_____

Date Read

Author _____ ☐ _____

Title_____

Referred by_____

Notes_____

_____

_____

_____

_____

_____

"*There is a great deal of difference between*
an eager man who wants to read a book
and a tired man who wants a book to read."

—G. K. Chesterton

Date Read

Author _____ ☐ _____

Title_____

Referred by_____

Notes_____

_____

_____

_____

_____

Date Read

Author _____ ☐ _____

Title_____

Referred by_____

Notes_____

_____

_____

_____

_____

Date Read

Author _____ ☐ _____

Title_____

Referred by_____

Notes_____

_____

_____

_____

_____

Date Read

Author _____ ☐ _____

Title_____

Referred by_____

Notes_____

_____

_____

_____

_____

Author _____ ☐ Date Read _____
Title _____
Referred by _____
Notes _____
_____
_____
_____
_____

Author _____ ☐ Date Read _____
Title _____
Referred by _____
Notes _____
_____
_____
_____
_____

Author _____ ☐ Date Read _____
Title _____
Referred by _____
Notes _____
_____
_____
_____
_____

"I *love being a writer.*
What I can't stand
is the paper work."
—Peter DeVries

NOTES TO MYSELF

"*When I write, I aim in my mind not toward New York but toward a vague spot a little east of Kansas. I think of the books on library shelves, without their jackets, years old, and a countryish teen-aged boy finding them, and having them speak to him. The reviews, the stacks in Brentano's, are just hurdles to get over, to place the books on that shelf.*"

—John Updike

Date Read

Author _____ ☐ _____

Title _____

Referred by _____

Notes _____

_____

_____

_____

_____

Date Read

Author _____ ☐ _____

Title _____

Referred by _____

Notes _____

_____

_____

_____

_____

Date Read

Author _____ ☐ _____

Title _____

Referred by _____

Notes _____

_____

_____

_____

_____

Date Read

Author _____ ☐ _____

Title _____

Referred by _____

Notes _____

_____

_____

_____

_____

Date Read

Author _____ ☐ _____

Title_____

Referred by_____

Notes_____

_____

_____

_____

_____

Date Read

Author _____ ☐ _____

Title_____

Referred by_____

Notes_____

_____

_____

_____

_____

Date Read

Author _____ ☐ _____

Title_____

Referred by_____

Notes_____

_____

_____

_____

_____

"If you would understand your own age,
read the works of fiction produced in it. People
in disguise speak freely." —Arthur Helps

Author _____ ☐   Date Read
_____
Title_____
Referred by_____
Notes_____
_____
_____
_____
_____

Author _____ ☐   Date Read
_____
Title_____
Referred by_____
Notes_____
_____
_____
_____
_____

Author _____ ☐   Date Read
_____
Title_____
Referred by_____
Notes_____
_____
_____
_____
_____

Author _____ ☐   Date Read
_____
Title_____
Referred by_____
Notes_____
_____
_____
_____
_____

Date Read

Author _____ ☐ _____

Title _____

Referred by _____

Notes _____

_____

_____

_____

_____

Date Read

Author _____ ☐ _____

Title _____

Referred by _____

Notes _____

_____

_____

_____

_____

Date Read

Author _____ ☐ _____

Title _____

Referred by _____

Notes _____

_____

_____

_____

_____

"*They can't yank a novelist like they can a pitcher.*
A novelist has to go the full nine, even if it kills him."

—Ernest Hemingway

NOTES TO MYSELF

"When power leads man to arrogance, poetry reminds him of his limitations. When power narrows the area of man's concern, poetry reminds him of the richness and diversity of his existence. When power corrupts, poetry cleanses."

—President John F. Kennedy

Date Read

Author _____ ☐ _____

Title _____

Referred by _____

Notes _____

_____

_____

_____

_____

Date Read

Author _____ ☐ _____

Title _____

Referred by _____

Notes _____

_____

_____

_____

_____

Date Read

Author _____ ☐ _____

Title _____

Referred by _____

Notes _____

_____

_____

_____

_____

Date Read

Author _____ ☐ _____

Title _____

Referred by _____

Notes _____

_____

_____

_____

_____

Date Read

Author _____ ☐ _____

Title _____

Referred by _____

Notes _____

_____

_____

_____

_____

_____

Date Read

Author _____ ☐ _____

Title _____

Referred by _____

Notes _____

_____

_____

_____

_____

_____

Date Read

Author _____ ☐ _____

Title _____

Referred by _____

Notes _____

_____

_____

_____

_____

_____

"One always tends to overpraise a long book
because one has got through it."

—E.M. Forster

Date Read

Author _____ ☐ _____

Title_____

Referred by_____

Notes_____

_____

_____

_____

_____

_____

Date Read

Author _____ ☐ _____

Title_____

Referred by_____

Notes_____

_____

_____

_____

_____

_____

Date Read

Author _____ ☐ _____

Title_____

Referred by_____

Notes_____

_____

_____

_____

_____

_____

Date Read

Author _____ ☐ _____

Title_____

Referred by_____

Notes_____

_____

_____

_____

_____

Date Read

Author _____ ☐ _____

Title _____

Referred by _____

Notes _____

_____

_____

_____

_____

Date Read

Author _____ ☐ _____

Title _____

Referred by _____

Notes _____

_____

_____

_____

_____

Date Read

Author _____ ☐ _____

Title _____

Referred by _____

Notes _____

_____

_____

_____

_____

"Where is human nature so weak as in the book store!"

—Henry Ward Beecher

Notes to Myself

I

"Often while reading a book one feels that the author would have preferred to paint rather than write; one can sense the pleasure he derives from describing a landscape or a person, as if he were painting what he is saying, because deep in his heart he would have preferred to use brushes and colors."

—Pablo Picasso

Date Read

Author _____ ☐ _____

Title _____

Referred by _____

Notes _____

_____

_____

_____

_____

Date Read

Author _____ ☐ _____

Title _____

Referred by _____

Notes _____

_____

_____

_____

_____

Date Read

Author _____ ☐ _____

Title _____

Referred by _____

Notes _____

_____

_____

_____

_____

Date Read

Author _____ ☐ _____

Title _____

Referred by _____

Notes _____

_____

_____

_____

_____

Date Read

Author _____ ☐ _____

Title_____

Referred by_____

Notes_____

_____

_____

_____

_____

Date Read

Author _____ ☐ _____

Title_____

Referred by_____

Notes_____

_____

_____

_____

_____

Date Read

Author _____ ☐ _____

Title_____

Referred by_____

Notes_____

_____

_____

_____

_____

"Books are good enough in their own way,
but they are a mighty bloodless substitute for life."

—Robert Louis Stevenson

Notes to Myself

"I *have long felt that any reviewer who expresses rage and loathing for a novel is preposterous. He or she is like a person who has put on full armor and attacked a hot fudge sundae or a banana split.*"

—Kurt Vonnegut, Jr.

Date Read

Author _____ ☐ _____

Title_____

Referred by_____

Notes_____

_____

_____

_____

_____

Date Read

Author _____ ☐ _____

Title_____

Referred by_____

Notes_____

_____

_____

_____

_____

Date Read

Author _____ ☐ _____

Title_____

Referred by_____

Notes_____

_____

_____

_____

_____

Date Read

Author _____ ☐ _____

Title_____

Referred by_____

Notes_____

_____

_____

_____

_____

Date Read

Author _____ ☐ _____

Title_____

Referred by_____

Notes_____

_____

_____

_____

_____

_____

Date Read

Author _____ ☐ _____

Title_____

Referred by_____

Notes_____

_____

_____

_____

_____

_____

Date Read

Author _____ ☐ _____

Title_____

Referred by_____

Notes_____

_____

_____

_____

_____

_____

"His books are selling like wildfire.
Everybody's burning them!"

—George DeWitt

Author _____ ☐ Date Read
                                                _____
Title _____
Referred by _____
Notes _____
_____
_____
_____
_____
_____

Author _____ ☐ Date Read
                                                _____
Title _____
Referred by _____
Notes _____
_____
_____
_____
_____
_____

Author _____ ☐ Date Read
                                                _____
Title _____
Referred by _____
Notes _____
_____
_____
_____
_____
_____

Author _____ ☐ Date Read
                                                _____
Title _____
Referred by _____
Notes _____
_____
_____
_____
_____

Date Read

Author _____ ☐ _____

Title _____

Referred by _____

Notes _____

_____

_____

_____

_____

_____

Date Read

Author _____ ☐ _____

Title _____

Referred by _____

Notes _____

_____

_____

_____

_____

_____

Date Read

Author _____ ☐ _____

Title _____

Referred by _____

Notes _____

_____

_____

_____

_____

_____

"Good prose is like a windowpane."

—George Orwell

Notes to Myself

"When you're a writer, you no longer see things with the freshness of the normal person. There are always two figures that work inside you, and if you are at all intelligent you realize that you have lost something. But I think there has always been this dichotomy in a real writer. He wants to be terribly human, and he responds emotionally; and at the same time there's this cold observer who cannot cry."

—Brian Moore

Author _____ ❏   Date Read
                                                _____
Title _____

Referred by _____

Notes _____

_____

_____

_____

_____

Author _____ ❏   Date Read
                                                _____
Title _____

Referred by _____

Notes _____

_____

_____

_____

_____

Author _____ ❏   Date Read
                                                _____
Title _____

Referred by _____

Notes _____

_____

_____

_____

_____

Author _____ ❏   Date Read
                                                _____
Title _____

Referred by _____

Notes _____

_____

_____

_____

_____

Date Read

Author _____ ❑ _____

Title_____

Referred by_____

Notes_____

_____

_____

_____

_____

Date Read

Author _____ ❑ _____

Title_____

Referred by_____

Notes_____

_____

_____

_____

_____

Date Read

Author _____ ❑ _____

Title_____

Referred by_____

Notes_____

_____

_____

_____

_____

"Reading is the sole means by which we slip,
involuntarily, often helplessly, into another's skin,
another's voice, another's soul."

—Joyce Carol Oates

Date Read

Author _____ ☐ _____

Title _____

Referred by _____

Notes _____

_____

_____

_____

_____

Date Read

Author _____ ☐ _____

Title _____

Referred by _____

Notes _____

_____

_____

_____

_____

Date Read

Author _____ ☐ _____

Title _____

Referred by _____

Notes _____

_____

_____

_____

_____

Date Read

Author _____ ☐ _____

Title _____

Referred by _____

Notes _____

_____

_____

_____

_____

Date Read

Author _____ ❏ _____

Title _____

Referred by _____

Notes _____

_____

_____

_____

_____

_____

Date Read

Author _____ ❏ _____

Title _____

Referred by _____

Notes _____

_____

_____

_____

_____

_____

Date Read

Author _____ ❏ _____

Title _____

Referred by _____

Notes _____

_____

_____

_____

_____

_____

"Books think for me."

—Charles Lamb

NOTES TO MYSELF

"I *finished my first book seventy six years ago. I offered it to every publisher on the English-speaking earth I had ever heard of. Their refusals were unanimous: and it did not get into print until, fifty years later, publishers would publish anything that had my name on it.*"

—George Bernard Shaw

Date Read

Author _____ ☐ _____

Title _____

Referred by _____

Notes _____

_____

_____

_____

_____

Date Read

Author _____ ☐ _____

Title _____

Referred by _____

Notes _____

_____

_____

_____

_____

Date Read

Author _____ ☐ _____

Title _____

Referred by _____

Notes _____

_____

_____

_____

_____

"Tis the good reader that makes the good book."

—Ralph Waldo Emerson

Date Read

Author _____ ☐ _____

Title _____

Referred by _____

Notes _____

_____

_____

_____

_____

Date Read

Author _____ ☐ _____

Title _____

Referred by _____

Notes _____

_____

_____

_____

_____

Date Read

Author _____ ☐ _____

Title _____

Referred by _____

Notes _____

_____

_____

_____

_____

Date Read

Author _____ ☐ _____

Title _____

Referred by _____

Notes _____

_____

_____

_____

_____

Date Read

Author _____ ❏ _____

Title _____

Referred by _____

Notes _____

_____

_____

_____

_____

Date Read

Author _____ ❏ _____

Title _____

Referred by _____

Notes _____

_____

_____

_____

_____

Date Read

Author _____ ❏ _____

Title _____

Referred by _____

Notes _____

_____

_____

_____

_____

Date Read

Author _____ ❏ _____

Title _____

Referred by _____

Notes _____

_____

_____

_____

_____

Date Read

Author _____ ❏ _____

Title _____

Referred by _____

Notes _____

_____

_____

_____

_____

Date Read

Author _____ ❏ _____

Title _____

Referred by _____

Notes _____

_____

_____

_____

_____

Date Read

Author _____ ❏ _____

Title _____

Referred by _____

Notes _____

_____

_____

_____

_____

"Books we must have though we lack bread."

—Alice Williams Brotherton

NOTES TO MYSELF

"A writer's problem does not change. He himself changes and the world changes, but his problem remains the same. It is always how to write truly and, having found out what is true, to project it in such a way that it becomes a part of the experience of the person who reads it."

—Ernest Hemingway

Author _____ ☐ Date Read
                                                       _____
Title _____
Referred by _____
Notes _____
_____
_____
_____
_____

Author _____ ☐ Date Read
                                                       _____
Title _____
Referred by _____
Notes _____
_____
_____
_____
_____

Author _____ ☐ Date Read
                                                       _____
Title _____
Referred by _____
Notes _____
_____
_____
_____
_____

Author _____ ☐ Date Read
                                                       _____
Title _____
Referred by _____
Notes _____
_____
_____
_____
_____

Date Read

Author _____ ☐ _____

Title _____

Referred by _____

Notes _____

_____

_____

_____

_____

_____

Date Read

Author _____ ☐ _____

Title _____

Referred by _____

Notes _____

_____

_____

_____

_____

Date Read

Author _____ ☐ _____

Title _____

Referred by _____

Notes _____

_____

_____

_____

_____

"I put things down on sheets of paper and stuff them in my pockets. When I have enough, I have a book."

—John Lennon

Date Read

Author _____ ☐ _____

Title _____

Referred by _____

Notes _____

_____

_____

_____

_____

_____

Date Read

Author _____ ☐ _____

Title _____

Referred by _____

Notes _____

_____

_____

_____

_____

_____

Date Read

Author _____ ☐ _____

Title _____

Referred by _____

Notes _____

_____

_____

_____

_____

_____

Date Read

Author _____ ☐ _____

Title _____

Referred by _____

Notes _____

_____

_____

_____

_____

_____

Date Read

Author _____ ☐ _____

Title_____

Referred by_____

Notes_____

_____

_____

_____

_____

Date Read

Author _____ ☐ _____

Title_____

Referred by_____

Notes_____

_____

_____

_____

_____

Date Read

Author _____ ☐ _____

Title_____

Referred by_____

Notes_____

_____

_____

_____

_____

"To read a writer is not merely to get an idea of what he says, but to go off with him, and travel in his company."

—André Gide

NOTES TO MYSELF

"The value of great fiction, we begin to suspect, is not that it entertains us or distracts us from our troubles, not just that it broadens our knowledge of people and places, but also that it helps us to know what we believe, reinforces the qualities that are noblest in us, leads us to feel uneasy about our failures and limitations."

—John Gardner

Date Read

Author _____ ☐ _____

Title _____

Referred by _____

Notes _____

_____

_____

_____

_____

Date Read

Author _____ ☐ _____

Title _____

Referred by _____

Notes _____

_____

_____

_____

_____

Date Read

Author _____ ☐ _____

Title _____

Referred by _____

Notes _____

_____

_____

_____

_____

Date Read

Author _____ ☐ _____

Title _____

Referred by _____

Notes _____

_____

_____

_____

_____

Author _____ ❏ Date Read _____

Title _____

Referred by _____

Notes _____

_____

_____

_____

_____

Author _____ ❏ Date Read _____

Title _____

Referred by _____

Notes _____

_____

_____

_____

_____

Author _____ ❏ Date Read _____

Title _____

Referred by _____

Notes _____

_____

_____

_____

_____

"A *room without books*
is like a body without a soul."

—Cicero

Date Read

Author _____ ☐ _____

Title _____

Referred by _____

Notes _____

_____

_____

_____

_____

Date Read

Author _____ ☐ _____

Title _____

Referred by _____

Notes _____

_____

_____

_____

_____

Date Read

Author _____ ☐ _____

Title _____

Referred by _____

Notes _____

_____

_____

_____

_____

Date Read

Author _____ ☐ _____

Title _____

Referred by _____

Notes _____

_____

_____

_____

_____

Date Read

Author _____ ☐ _____

Title_____

Referred by_____

Notes_____

_____

_____

_____

_____

Date Read

Author _____ ☐ _____

Title_____

Referred by_____

Notes_____

_____

_____

_____

_____

Date Read

Author _____ ☐ _____

Title_____

Referred by_____

Notes_____

_____

_____

_____

_____

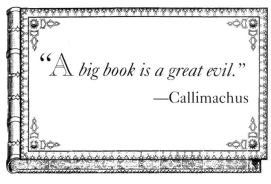

"A *big book is a great evil.*"

—Callimachus

NOTES TO MYSELF

"*Mostly we authors must repeat ourselves — that's the truth. We have two or three great moving experiences in our lives — experiences so great and moving it doesn't seem at the time that anyone else has been caught up and pounded and dazzled and astonished and beaten and broken and rescued and illuminated and rewarded and humbled in just that way ever before.*"

—F. Scott Fitzgerald

Date Read

Author _____ ☐ _____

Title_____

Referred by_____

Notes_____

_____

_____

_____

_____

Date Read

Author _____ ☐ _____

Title_____

Referred by_____

Notes_____

_____

_____

_____

_____

Date Read

Author _____ ☐ _____

Title_____

Referred by_____

Notes_____

_____

_____

_____

_____

Date Read

Author _____ ☐ _____

Title_____

Referred by_____

Notes_____

_____

_____

_____

_____

Date Read

Author _____ ☐ _____

Title _____

Referred by _____

Notes _____

_____

_____

_____

_____

Date Read

Author _____ ☐ _____

Title _____

Referred by _____

Notes _____

_____

_____

_____

_____

Date Read

Author _____ ☐ _____

Title _____

Referred by _____

Notes _____

_____

_____

_____

_____

"*A book is a garden carried in one's pocket.*"

—Chinese Proverb

Date Read

Author _____ ❏ _____

Title _____

Referred by _____

Notes _____

_____

_____

_____

_____

Date Read

Author _____ ❏ _____

Title _____

Referred by _____

Notes _____

_____

_____

_____

_____

Date Read

Author _____ ❏ _____

Title _____

Referred by _____

Notes _____

_____

_____

_____

_____

Date Read

Author _____ ❏ _____

Title _____

Referred by _____

Notes _____

_____

_____

_____

_____

Date Read

Author _____ ❏ _____

Title _____

Referred by _____

Notes _____

_____

_____

_____

_____

Date Read

Author _____ ❏ _____

Title _____

Referred by _____

Notes _____

_____

_____

_____

_____

Date Read

Author _____ ❏ _____

Title _____

Referred by _____

Notes _____

_____

_____

_____

_____

"*No woman was ever ruined
by a book.*"

—Mayor Jimmy Walker
New York City

Notes to Myself

"A *poem is never a put–up job....*
It begins as a lump in the throat, a sense
of wrong, a homesickness, a love sickness.
It is never a thought to begin with."

—Robert Frost

Author _____ ☐ Date Read _____

Title _____

Referred by _____

Notes _____

_____

_____

_____

_____

Author _____ ☐ Date Read _____

Title _____

Referred by _____

Notes _____

_____

_____

_____

_____

Author _____ ☐ Date Read _____

Title _____

Referred by _____

Notes _____

_____

_____

_____

_____

Author _____ ☐ Date Read _____

Title _____

Referred by _____

Notes _____

_____

_____

_____

_____

Date Read

Author _____ ❏ _____

Title _____

Referred by _____

Notes _____

_____

_____

_____

_____

Date Read

Author _____ ❏ _____

Title _____

Referred by _____

Notes _____

_____

_____

_____

_____

Date Read

Author _____ ❏ _____

Title _____

Referred by _____

Notes _____

_____

_____

_____

_____

"With sixty staring me in the face, I have developed inflammation of the sentence structure and a definite hardening of the paragraphs."

—James Thurber at 59

Date Read

Author _____ ☐ _____

Title _____

Referred by _____

Notes _____

_____

_____

_____

_____

Date Read

Author _____ ☐ _____

Title _____

Referred by _____

Notes _____

_____

_____

_____

_____

Date Read

Author _____ ☐ _____

Title _____

Referred by _____

Notes _____

_____

_____

_____

_____

Date Read

Author _____ ☐ _____

Title _____

Referred by _____

Notes _____

_____

_____

_____

_____

Date Read

Author _____ ☐ _____

Title _____

Referred by _____

Notes _____

_____

_____

_____

_____

_____

Date Read

Author _____ ☐ _____

Title _____

Referred by _____

Notes _____

_____

_____

_____

_____

_____

Date Read

Author _____ ☐ _____

Title _____

Referred by _____

Notes _____

_____

_____

_____

_____

_____

"*Come, my best friends, my best books, and lead me on.*"

—Abraham Cowley

Notes to Myself

"*I suggest that the only books that influence us are those for which we are ready, and which have gone a little farther down our particular path than we have yet gone ourselves.*"

—E.M. Forster

Author _____ ❏ Date Read _____

Title _____

Referred by _____

Notes _____

_____

_____

_____

_____

_____

Author _____ ❏ Date Read _____

Title _____

Referred by _____

Notes _____

_____

_____

_____

_____

_____

Author _____ ❏ Date Read _____

Title _____

Referred by _____

Notes _____

_____

_____

_____

_____

_____

Author _____ ❏ Date Read _____

Title _____

Referred by _____

Notes _____

_____

_____

_____

_____

Date Read

Author _____ ☐ _____

Title_____

Referred by_____

Notes_____

_____

_____

_____

_____

Date Read

Author _____ ☐ _____

Title_____

Referred by_____

Notes_____

_____

_____

_____

_____

Date Read

Author _____ ☐ _____

Title_____

Referred by_____

Notes_____

_____

_____

_____

_____

"The pleasure of all reading is doubled when one lives with another who shares the same books."

—Katherine Mansfield

NOTES TO MYSELF

"An author is a person who can never take innocent pleasure in visiting a bookstore again. Say you go in and discover that there are no copies of your book on the shelves. You resent all the other books—I don't care if they are Great Expectations, Life on the Mississippi *and the* King James Bible *that are on the shelves."*

—Roy Blount, Jr.

Date Read

Author _____ ❑ _____

Title_____

Referred by_____

Notes_____

_____

_____

_____

_____

_____

Date Read

Author _____ ❑ _____

Title_____

Referred by_____

Notes_____

_____

_____

_____

_____

_____

Date Read

Author _____ ❑ _____

Title_____

Referred by_____

Notes_____

_____

_____

_____

_____

_____

Date Read

Author _____ ❑ _____

Title_____

Referred by_____

Notes_____

_____

_____

_____

_____

_____

Date Read

Author _____ ❑ _____

Title _____

Referred by _____

Notes _____

_____

_____

_____

_____

Date Read

Author _____ ❑ _____

Title _____

Referred by _____

Notes _____

_____

_____

_____

_____

Date Read

Author _____ ❑ _____

Title _____

Referred by _____

Notes _____

_____

_____

_____

_____

"I *divide all readers into two classes—those who read to remember and those who read to forget.*"

—E.M. Forster

Date Read

Author _____ ☐ _____

Title _____

Referred by _____

Notes _____

_____

_____

_____

_____

Date Read

Author _____ ☐ _____

Title _____

Referred by _____

Notes _____

_____

_____

_____

_____

Date Read

Author _____ ☐ _____

Title _____

Referred by _____

Notes _____

_____

_____

_____

_____

Date Read

Author _____ ☐ _____

Title _____

Referred by _____

Notes _____

_____

_____

_____

_____

Date Read

Author _____ ☐ _____

Title _____

Referred by _____

Notes _____

_____

_____

_____

_____

Date Read

Author _____ ☐ _____

Title _____

Referred by _____

Notes _____

_____

_____

_____

_____

Date Read

Author _____ ☐ _____

Title _____

Referred by _____

Notes _____

_____

_____

_____

_____

"*The difference between the right word and the almost right word is the difference between the lightning and the lightning bug.*"

—Mark Twain

NOTES TO MYSELF

"*Never dare tell me again anything about 'green grass'. Tell me how the lawn was flecked with shadows. I know perfectly well that grass is green. So does everybody else in England.... Make me see what it was that made your garden distinct from a thousand others.*"
—Robert Louis Stevenson

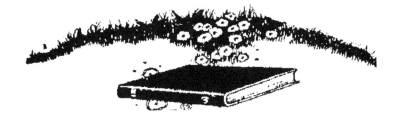

Author _____ ☐ Date Read _____

Title _____

Referred by _____

Notes _____

_____

_____

_____

_____

Author _____ ☐ Date Read _____

Title _____

Referred by _____

Notes _____

_____

_____

_____

_____

Author _____ ☐ Date Read _____

Title _____

Referred by _____

Notes _____

_____

_____

_____

_____

Author _____ ☐ Date Read _____

Title _____

Referred by _____

Notes _____

_____

_____

_____

_____

Date Read

Author _____ ☐ _____

Title _____

Referred by _____

Notes _____

_____

_____

_____

_____

Date Read

Author _____ ☐ _____

Title _____

Referred by _____

Notes _____

_____

_____

_____

_____

Date Read

Author _____ ☐ _____

Title _____

Referred by _____

Notes _____

_____

_____

_____

_____

"$\mathbb{R}$*eading, not just an escape,*
but an exercise in living..."

—Taylor Caldwell

Date Read

Author _____ ❑ _____

Title _____

Referred by _____

Notes _____

_____

_____

_____

_____

Date Read

Author _____ ❑ _____

Title _____

Referred by _____

Notes _____

_____

_____

_____

_____

Date Read

Author _____ ❑ _____

Title _____

Referred by _____

Notes _____

_____

_____

_____

_____

Date Read

Author _____ ❑ _____

Title _____

Referred by _____

Notes _____

_____

_____

_____

_____

Date Read

Author _____ ☐ _____

Title _____

Referred by _____

Notes _____

_____

_____

_____

_____

_____

Date Read

Author _____ ☐ _____

Title _____

Referred by _____

Notes _____

_____

_____

_____

_____

_____

Date Read

Author _____ ☐ _____

Title _____

Referred by _____

Notes _____

_____

_____

_____

_____

_____

"A *classic is something that everybody wants to have*
read and nobody wants to read."

—Mark Twain

Date Read

Author _____ ☐ _____

Title _____

Referred by _____

Notes _____

_____

_____

_____

_____

Date Read

Author _____ ☐ _____

Title _____

Referred by _____

Notes _____

_____

_____

_____

_____

Date Read

Author _____ ☐ _____

Title _____

Referred by _____

Notes _____

_____

_____

_____

_____

Date Read

Author _____ ☐ _____

Title _____

Referred by _____

Notes _____

_____

_____

_____

_____

Date Read

Author _____ ☐ _____

Title _____

Referred by _____

Notes _____

_____

_____

_____

_____

Date Read

Author _____ ☐ _____

Title _____

Referred by _____

Notes _____

_____

_____

_____

_____

Date Read

Author _____ ☐ _____

Title _____

Referred by _____

Notes _____

_____

_____

_____

_____

"You* know how it is*
in the kid's book world.
It's just bunny eat bunny."

—Anonymous

NOTES TO MYSELF

"*A person who publishes a book willfully appears before the populace with his pants down.... If it is a good book, nothing can hurt him. If it is a bad book, nothing can help him.*"

—Edna St. Vincent Millay

Date Read

Author _____ ☐ _____

Title _____

Referred by _____

Notes _____

_____

_____

_____

_____

Date Read

Author _____ ☐ _____

Title _____

Referred by _____

Notes _____

_____

_____

_____

_____

Date Read

Author _____ ☐ _____

Title _____

Referred by _____

Notes _____

_____

_____

_____

_____

Date Read

Author _____ ☐ _____

Title _____

Referred by _____

Notes _____

_____

_____

_____

_____

Date Read

Author _____ ❏ _____

Title_____

Referred by_____

Notes_____

_____

_____

_____

_____

_____

Date Read

Author _____ ❏ _____

Title_____

Referred by_____

Notes_____

_____

_____

_____

_____

_____

Date Read

Author _____ ❏ _____

Title_____

Referred by_____

Notes_____

_____

_____

_____

_____

_____

"Insects sting, not in malice, but because they want to live.

It is the same with critics;

they desire our blood, not our pain."

—Friedrich Nietzsche

Date Read

Author _____ ☐ _____

Title _____

Referred by _____

Notes _____

_____

_____

_____

_____

Date Read

Author _____ ☐ _____

Title _____

Referred by _____

Notes _____

_____

_____

_____

_____

Date Read

Author _____ ☐ _____

Title _____

Referred by _____

Notes _____

_____

_____

_____

_____

Date Read

Author _____ ☐ _____

Title _____

Referred by _____

Notes _____

_____

_____

_____

_____

Date Read

Author _____ ☐ _____

Title_____

Referred by_____

Notes_____

_____

_____

_____

_____

Date Read

Author _____ ☐ _____

Title_____

Referred by_____

Notes_____

_____

_____

_____

_____

Date Read

Author _____ ☐ _____

Title_____

Referred by_____

Notes_____

_____

_____

_____

_____

"There are books...which rank
in our life with parents and lovers
and passionate experiences."

—Ralph Walso Emerson

Date Read

Author _____ ☐ _____

Title _____

Referred by _____

Notes _____

_____

_____

_____

_____

Date Read

Author _____ ☐ _____

Title _____

Referred by _____

Notes _____

_____

_____

_____

_____

Date Read

Author _____ ☐ _____

Title _____

Referred by _____

Notes _____

_____

_____

_____

_____

Date Read

Author _____ ☐ _____

Title _____

Referred by _____

Notes _____

_____

_____

_____

_____

Author _____ ☐ **Date Read** _____

Title _____

Referred by _____

Notes _____

_____

_____

_____

_____

_____

Author _____ ☐ **Date Read** _____

Title _____

Referred by _____

Notes _____

_____

_____

_____

_____

_____

Author _____ ☐ **Date Read** _____

Title _____

Referred by _____

Notes _____

_____

_____

_____

_____

_____

"The Agee woman told us for three quarters of an hour how she came to write her beastly book, when a simple apology was all that was required..."

—P.J. Wodehouse

NOTES TO MYSELF

"*Everybody has their own idea of what's a poet. Robert Frost, President Johnson, T.S. Eliot, Rudolph Valentino—they're all poets. I like to think of myself as the one who carries the light bulb.*"

—Bob Dylan

Date Read

Author _____ □

Title _____

Referred by _____

Notes _____

_____

_____

_____

_____

Date Read

Author _____ □

Title _____

Referred by _____

Notes _____

_____

_____

_____

_____

Date Read

Author _____ □

Title _____

Referred by _____

Notes _____

_____

_____

_____

_____

Date Read

Author _____ □

Title _____

Referred by _____

Notes _____

_____

_____

_____

_____

Date Read
Author _____ ☐ _____
Title_____
Referred by_____
Notes_____
_____
_____
_____
_____

Date Read
Author _____ ☐ _____
Title_____
Referred by_____
Notes_____
_____
_____
_____
_____

Date Read
Author _____ ☐ _____
Title_____
Referred by_____
Notes_____
_____
_____
_____
_____

"*If you ask me what I have come to do in this world,*
I who am an artist,
I will reply, 'I am here to live aloud.'"

—Emile Zola

Notes to Myself

"Outside of a dog,
a book is a man's best friend;
Inside of a dog,
it's too dark to read."

—Groucho Marx

Date Read

Author _____ ☐ _____

Title _____

Referred by _____

Notes _____

_____

_____

_____

_____

Date Read

Author _____ ☐ _____

Title _____

Referred by _____

Notes _____

_____

_____

_____

_____

Date Read

Author _____ ☐ _____

Title _____

Referred by _____

Notes _____

_____

_____

_____

_____

Date Read

Author _____ ☐ _____

Title _____

Referred by _____

Notes _____

_____

_____

_____

_____

Date Read

Author _____ ☐ _____

Title_____

Referred by_____

Notes_____

_____

_____

_____

_____

Date Read

Author _____ ☐ _____

Title_____

Referred by_____

Notes_____

_____

_____

_____

_____

Date Read

Author _____ ☐ _____

Title_____

Referred by_____

Notes_____

_____

_____

_____

_____

"When I am dead, I hope it will be said:
'His sins were scarlet but his books were read.'"

—Hilaire Belloc

NOTES TO MYSELF

"*Every man who knows how to read has it in his power to magnify himself, to multiply the ways in which he exists, to make his life full, significant and interesting.*"

—Aldous Huxley

Date Read

Author _____ ☐ _____

Title _____

Referred by _____

Notes _____

_____

_____

_____

_____

Date Read

Author _____ ☐ _____

Title _____

Referred by _____

Notes _____

_____

_____

_____

_____

Date Read

Author _____ ☐ _____

Title _____

Referred by _____

Notes _____

_____

_____

_____

_____

Date Read

Author _____ ☐ _____

Title _____

Referred by _____

Notes _____

_____

_____

_____

_____

Author _____ ❏   Date Read _____

Title_____

Referred by_____

Notes_____

_____

_____

_____

_____

Author _____ ❏   Date Read _____

Title_____

Referred by_____

Notes_____

_____

_____

_____

_____

Author _____ ❏   Date Read _____

Title_____

Referred by_____

Notes_____

_____

_____

_____

_____

"True ease in writing comes from art, not chance,
As those move easiest who have learned to dance."

—Alexander Pope

Date Read

Author _____ ☐ _____

Title_____

Referred by_____

Notes_____

_____

_____

_____

_____

Date Read

Author _____ ☐ _____

Title_____

Referred by_____

Notes_____

_____

_____

_____

_____

Date Read

Author _____ ☐ _____

Title_____

Referred by_____

Notes_____

_____

_____

_____

_____

Date Read

Author _____ ☐ _____

Title_____

Referred by_____

Notes_____

_____

_____

_____

_____

Author _____ ❏ Date Read ___
Title_____
Referred by_____
Notes_____
_____
_____
_____
_____

Author _____ ❏ Date Read ___
Title_____
Referred by_____
Notes_____
_____
_____
_____
_____

Author _____ ❏ Date Read ___
Title_____
Referred by_____
Notes_____
_____
_____
_____
_____

"$\mathbb{A}$ *writer often does not begin to live until*
he has been dead for some time."

—Rudyard Kipling

Date Read

Author _____ ☐ _____

Title_____

Referred by_____

Notes_____

_____

_____

_____

_____

Date Read

Author _____ ☐ _____

Title_____

Referred by_____

Notes_____

_____

_____

_____

_____

Date Read

Author _____ ☐ _____

Title_____

Referred by_____

Notes_____

_____

_____

_____

_____

Date Read

Author _____ ☐ _____

Title_____

Referred by_____

Notes_____

_____

_____

_____

_____

Date Read

Author _____ ☐ _____

Title _____

Referred by _____

Notes _____

_____

_____

_____

_____

_____

Date Read

Author _____ ☐ _____

Title _____

Referred by _____

Notes _____

_____

_____

_____

_____

_____

Date Read

Author _____ ☐ _____

Title _____

Referred by _____

Notes _____

_____

_____

_____

_____

_____

> " A great book should leave you with many
> experiences, and slightly exhausted at the end.
> You live several lives while reading."
>
> —William Styron

NOTES TO MYSELF

XYZ

On being asked what condition of man he considered most pitiable: "A lonesome man on a rainy day who does not know how to read."

—Ben Franklin

Wisdom and Foibles of the Great

Author _____ ❑ Date Read _____
Title _____
Referred by _____
Notes _____
_____
_____
_____
_____

Author _____ ❑ Date Read _____
Title _____
Referred by _____
Notes _____
_____
_____
_____
_____

Author _____ ❑ Date Read _____
Title _____
Referred by _____
Notes _____
_____
_____
_____
_____

Author _____ ❑ Date Read _____
Title _____
Referred by _____
Notes _____
_____
_____
_____
_____

Date Read ❑ _____

Author _____

Title _____

Referred by _____

Notes _____

_____

_____

_____

_____

Date Read ❑ _____

Author _____

Title _____

Referred by _____

Notes _____

_____

_____

_____

_____

Date Read ❑ _____

Author _____

Title _____

Referred by _____

Notes _____

_____

_____

_____

_____

"*Of making many books there is no end.*"
—Ecclesiastes 12:12

Notes to Myself